For Maurice

OLIVER

and his

ALLIGATOR

PAUL SCHMID

 • HYPERION BOOKS

NEW YORK

Oliver sometimes felt his *brave*
wasn't nearly as big
as he needed it to be.

So on his first day of school,
Oliver thought it best to stop by
the swamp and pick up an alligator.

Just in case things got rough.

It got rough *right* away.

A lady who wasn't his mom said,
"Welcome to your new school!
What might your name be?"

Oliver suddenly couldn't
remember his name was Oliver.
So he said: *"Munch, munch!"*

Oliver's alligator swallowed the lady.

Oliver walked into the classroom.

A girl came up to Oliver.
"Hi!" she said.
"My name is Grace,
and I love *bunnies*!
What do you love?"

Oliver really wanted
to say "turtles," but
the word got stuck
and stayed inside.

Oliver could say
"Munch, munch!"
so his alligator
swallowed the girl.

Oliver was beginning to
feel better about school.

But there were so many
other children there!

They were all very noisy
and made Oliver nervous.

Oliver wondered
if they all could fit.

They could.

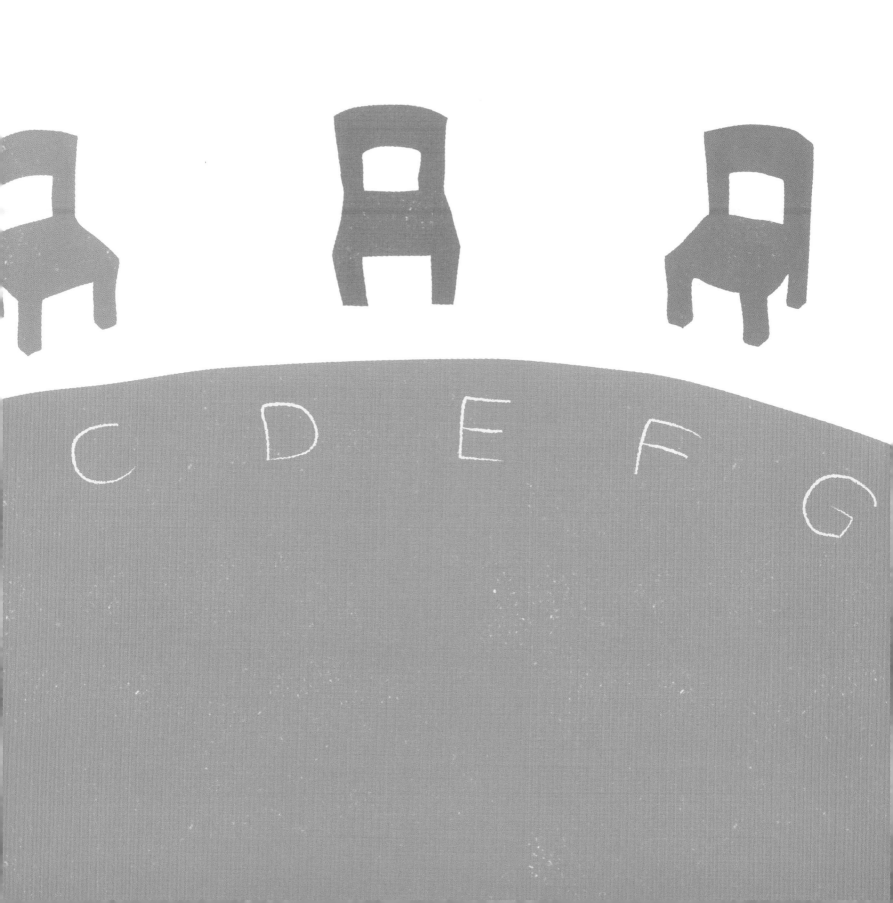

It was certainly
much quieter now!

Oliver sat down.

The teacher had put up brightly colored decorations.
Would Oliver have to learn everything there is?

"*Munch, munch!*"
Oliver whispered.

He waited for school to start.

School is maybe
kind of a little *boring*,
thought Oliver.

Then Oliver heard singing.

And laughing.

And *fun*!

It came
from *inside*
his alligator.

They were
having school.

Without Oliver!

"But!" said Oliver.

"Wait!" said Oliver.

"Munch, munch!"

First Edition
10 9 8 7 6 5 4 3 2 1
H106-9333-5-13074

Printed in Malaysia
The art is created with pastel pencil and digital color.

Library of Congress Cataloging-in-Publication Data

Schmid, Paul.
Oliver and his alligator / Paul Schmid.
p. cm.
Summary: Nervous about the first day of school, Oliver brings an alligator to school for protection.
ISBN 978-1-4231-7437-0
[1. First day of school—Fiction. 2. Schools—Fiction. 3. Fear—Fiction. 4. Alligators—Fiction.] I. Title.
PZ7.S3492Ol 2013
[E]—dc23   2012020298.

Reinforced binding
Visit www.disneyhyperionbooks.com